MAX

THE RIFTS OF TIME

Micaiah J. Lukalu

Copyright © 2024

Micaiah J. Lukalu

All rights reserved. This book or any portion thereof may not be reproduced or used in any manner whatsoever without the express written permission of the publisher except for the use of brief quotations in a book review.

ISBN: 9798321396728

Edited and Designed by KayVee Books

I want to dedicate this book to my Lord and Saviour, Jesus Christ because without His grace and mercy this would not have been possible.

CONTENTS

	Acknowledgments	i
	Prologue	1
1	Chapter One	3
2	Chapter Two	7
3	Chapter Three	12
4	Chapter Four	17
5	Chapter Five	22
6	Chapter Six	28
7	Chapter Seven	37
8	Chapter Eight	44
9	Chapter Nine	52
10	Chapter Ten	55
	About The Author	61

ACKNOWLEDGMENTS

My mum for always supporting me. My grandma for encouraging to keep pushing and not give up, uncle Emmanuel for encouraging me to start writing and my English teacher (Mrs Begum) for telling me that anything is possible

PROLOGUE

There it was, his body floating in what seemed like space. Max, with a peculiar expression, noticed a small pimple burgeoning on his face, just above his left eyebrow—not too pretty, to say the least. He wondered how he could see his body without a mirror or any means to reflect his image. Looking down at himself, he realised he was dead, his soul observing his lifeless form, but how? He had felt no pain, only a sense of detachment. Unfortunately, that feeling was short-lived as Max began to experience a tugging sensation. He was being pulled back into his body, but why? He didn't want to return; he preferred the freedom of his spirit to the confinement of his clumsy, nonsensical human form. Max fought as hard as he could, a valiant effort, but it was futile against the force drawing him back. Reluctantly, Max allowed himself to be brought back home.

CHAPTER 1

"Max, hurry! The clock is ticking, and time is short," whispered the round timepiece.

It shone with a sort of ethereal, otherworldly light. Its face was highly sophisticated: dials here, knobs there. It was like nothing had ever been seen before, and Maxwell Levi Junior somehow felt connected to this strange anomaly.

Slowly and carefully, Max stretched out his hand to touch it. So close. Nearly there.

"Wake up!"

Max was awoken by the shrill shriek of his mother's voice telling him to wake up. She never let him sleep past nine o'clock, but what could he do except obey, for the Bible says to honour your father and mother? His mother had told him to shower and get dressed because they would be cleaning out his dad's garage today.

It had been a while since his father had disappeared, presumed dead. He was on an expedition in the Alps, trying to find evidence that giants were real and once walked upon the land, but he never returned. Max and his mother had waited, but they had to accept that the man they loved was never returning. It had been nearly a year now since the disappearance of Maxwell Senior, but it was still fresh and also painful enough that it hurt to talk about him. Max's mouth dropped, and his eyes bulged; it was a big surprise to hear that his mother was ready to take on such a big task. But as he walked, he said that no matter how hard this job may be, he would stand by his mother's side and keep her strong. The garage was huge, and as soon as Max stepped foot in it, he knew taming this beast would be no easy feat. Knowing his mother so well, this job could take weeks, but Max knew they would be done in days if not hours.

"Start with the letters, separate the junk from the business, then put them into the filing cupboard at the back," whispered his mother, Anne, with a quavering voice.

There were enough letters to fill up the trunk of a gigantic car completely; however, Max was ready to take on any challenge that came his way.

At first glance, Maxwell Senior appeared very civilised, organised, and tidy but looks can be deceiving. There were things everywhere: bits of paper, metal, and screwdrivers on the floor; cobwebs everywhere; even a bird's nest wedged between a pile of miscellaneous boxes and, for some reason, a wardrobe. Around mid-afternoon, Max found something exciting that would change his life forever, but of course, he didn't know that yet. In the humongous pile of random letters, one small brown envelope was addressed to Max, which was strange; he never got letters for anything, not even from his friends—everything was sent digitally. He thought about opening it but was reluctant. What if it was something silly that his friends had sent him? Before he could think about it too much, he opened the envelope.

Slowly. Carefully. Nearly there...

CHAPTER 2

A key and a Post-it note? What the heck, this was definitely a prank, thought Max. Who would put a Post-it note and a key in an envelope? What was the point? The post-it note read: "Hurry, you must save me. Time is running out. Use the key to find the artefact. You must find it. It's closer than you think but further than you know. Dad."

Max was baffled. Key, monument, save me, Dad? What kind of sick joke was this? Whoever had written that note had even gone to the lengths of providing an actual key. There was no way it could be real. His Dad was dead, and dead people didn't suddenly start writing notes and sending people random keys. But wait, as Max held the key in his hand, he felt a sense of familiarity and stopped to examine it properly. It was gold with silver veins running across it, and on the handle of the key were the initials M.S.

Maxwell Senior? It couldn't be, could it? Could there maybe be a chance that his father was alive? That was impossible. Maxwell's father had been dead for nearly a year now, but there was only one way to find out. His Dad kept a safe hidden somewhere in the same garage Max and his mother were cleaning. If Max could find it, he could figure out whether or not his father was still alive.

"What are you doing?" said Max's mother.

Anne loomed over Max with a curious but slightly ticke-doff expression. Max quickly crumpled the mysterious note and hid it in his pocket because he had decided to tell his mother nothing until he had proper evidence.

"Nothing, Mum, just found this key. I think it's from Dad's safe. Do you know where it is?"

His mother pointed stiffly to a pile of files and folders. Behind them was the safe, which looked like it had been through the wars. It was dented, bashed, and beaten—almost as if someone had tried to break it open but failed several times. But Max thought nothing of it.

It was dinner time, but all Max could think about was the safe. He had not opened it because he did not want his mother to ask questions, so he had decided to go back after dinner when his mother was busy watching her favourite TV show. Dinner was usually quiet, simply because there was nothing to talk about. Since Maxwell Senior disappeared, a rift had appeared between them and continued growing to the point where they could be in the same room and not even talk.

He was back in the garage. The safe was right there, calling out to him. He pulled out the key from his left pocket. This was the moment of truth, the decider. He placed the key in the lock. It turned once, twice. CLICK. The door of the safe scraped across the floor and made a bit too much noise for Max's liking. He quickly looked around him, not wanting to be caught unaware like earlier. The inside of the safe was not as Max had expected it to be. There was no money or gold or anything interesting, really. But there was one thing that confused Max: there was a small circular watch inside the safe, but it was the same watch Max had seen in his dream that morning, except it wasn't glowing. How could this be possible? There was no way this could happen; things people saw in their dreams did not just appear in real life. That wasn't how the world worked. He wanted to turn and run, never looking back, but for some reason, he couldn't. He was rooted to the spot. He felt like some powerful force was stopping him from moving. He stared at the watch. It stared back at him, calling to him. Wait, no, that can't be. Watches didn't speak; they were inanimate objects. They were not alive, and they never were.

The impulse was too great. Max felt that he had to touch this strange contraption. Without realising it, his hand was in the air, inches away.

"Don't touch it!"

Max heard his mother's running footsteps behind him. Before she could reach him, he closed the gap between his fingers and the watch.

Blinding light. Max could not see; he was bathed in a light blue glow. His mother was nowhere to be seen. The only thing that Max could see was the watch. It looked exactly like it had in his dream, and the other thing he could see was his Dad.

CHAPTER 3

Max's father was there. In the flesh? Well, not exactly; his spirit was there, talking to Max, but Max was not listening because he could hear his dad's voice for the first time in ages.

"Max! Snap out of it. Yes, I'm here. I'm alive, but you can think about that later. Right now, I need you to listen. This watch that you see is no ordinary watch. It is a time-travelling device. Yes, I said time-travelling. Now, I have managed to get stuck between time and nothingness. I need you to save me before my cells are shredded apart. The watch will guide you."

That was it. No "I love you" or "I've missed you," but he was grateful that he had been able to see his dad again, even if it was in a really weird way. The light was gone. He was back in the garage, but wait, where was his mother? He listened carefully and realised he could hear his mother's footsteps approaching the garage door. He quickly grabbed the watch, closed the door to the safe, and pretended to be looking for something.

"What are you doing in here? You should be in bed." What? Max was extremely confused. Hadn't his mum been in here and shouted at him not to touch the watch? He checked the time on the clock behind him: 9:15. When he had entered the garage, it had been 9:13. His mother had come crashing in ten minutes later, 9:23, which meant that, somehow, Maxwell Junior had returned in time. But how?

Of course, it was the watch! This meant that everything his dad had said was true and was not just a figment of his imagination. Wow, this was shell-shocking. Amazing! Time travel was real. But then something dawned on Max: if he had gone back in time, then that meant that his father was really in danger, and it was up to Max to save him. "Erm, nothing, Ma, just looking for some coins I dropped earlier. Goodnight." Max walked past his mother hurriedly, hoping that she would not notice the mysterious bulge in his pocket, but much to Max's luck, she didn't.

Another night, another dream. The watch could communicate with Max through dreams, although Max hadn't realised this yet and remained as oblivious as ever to the dire circumstances of his situation. The watch realises that, for Max to understand his role fully, he has to be shown exactly what would happen if he failed to find and rescue his father.

There was rubble everywhere. Something terrible had happened, something very bad. Dead bodies lay strewn across the ground like rag-dolls. The sky looked as if it had been ripped open by God Himself, but the silence was the one thing that was totally out of place. There was no sound, no sound at all. What had happened? Why had this happened?

There he was, throwing it away, rejecting his

destiny, refusing to save the one who needed him most. He had made the world like this. He had killed everyone. He was the reason it was so quiet. Maxwell Junior had destroyed the world that he was supposed to save. Maxwell had refused to accept his destiny, and because of that, destruction had engulfed the world, and the whole space-time continuum had collapsed. How could one tiny person have the power to destroy the entire galaxy? Well, the answer is he could destroy everything because he had complete power over time and space and neglected to do the right thing, and now he would pay the consequences. His family would be first, then his friends, then the people he knew, and the whole world would follow. There was only one thing that Max could do to stop this tragedy from happening, and that was for him to buckle up and get ready for an explosive ride ahead.

Max woke up earlier than usual. He had just had a terrible dream, something about Armageddon and how if he didn't save his dad, the world would be destroyed. It couldn't have just been a random dream, he thought. He would have forgotten about it before waking up if it was. This had to be a sign, some sort of call to action. Suddenly, Max knew what he had to do. After getting ready, he went downstairs to the kitchen and almost completely emptied its contents into his rucksack. Then came the moment of truth. Carefully and cautiously, he pulled out the watch. The strap was like any other, with a simple buckle to fasten it. He pulled the watch as tight as it would go so it was nice and secure. Now what? Nothing was happening, at least that's what Max thought, until a weird beam of phone light shot out of the watch and scanned his face.

"Maxwell Junior." Max had almost jumped out of his skin.

The watch had spoken his name in the creepiest robotic voice ever, but now something was happening. The cogs and knobs were turning; the watch was getting warmer and warmer, then Max started getting dizzy. The world was spinning around him. He was no longer in the kitchen. He was at the Eiffel Tower. Wait, no, he was at the Tower of Babel. Wait, no, he was outside a Roman fort.

CHAPTER 4

"I have been waiting a long time to see you, Maxwell," Max looked around anxiously, trying to search for the owner of that voice, but ended up vomiting his breakfast on the lush green grass instead. A dark shadow appeared over Max, and he felt a soft hand on his back. "Take a deep breath; everybody vomits on their first time, but you'll get used to it. Don't worry." Max looked at this kind man standing over him and felt a sense of déjà vu.

Then it hit him; this man was his dad's expedition partner, "Uncle Phineas, is that you?" The man Max had just addressed wore clothes that looked very out of place to Max. He wore Roman armour, a silver breastplate and shoulder pads, and a meter-long sword at his hip. He wore reddish armour-plated trousers and a pair of worn brown sandals on his lower half. "It's been a long time since we last saw each other, hasn't it?" spoke Max's Uncle. At this point, Max was hungry and just wanted to be left alone so he could think. He had just done something that most people could only dream of doing, but that would not happen anytime soon. His Uncle wanted to chat with Max and explain what needed to be done because there was no time to dilly-dally. The Roman fort was surprisingly modern. It still looked ancient, but there were a few things that didn't belong in this era, like the 55-inch TV that was mounted on the left wall of the inner building inside the fort, and there was also, for some reason, a whole room of billiard tables. Max was learning new things about his Uncle every second.

"Like your dad, you are a Time Warper. Yes, you heard me, a Time Warper. Our job is to travel through time and prevent any and all catastrophic events from happening, but the one thing we never do is use our time-travelling devices for personal pleasure. Each Time Warper will get their own personal and customised teleportation device. But only if they pass the initiation test, which you, Max, happen to have just done by coming here to this time and place."

Max was seriously struggling to take all that information in. So, what Uncle Phineas was trying to say was that there was a whole group of people called Time Warpers, and basically, they protected the space-time thingy. Max was buzzing with crazy ecstatic energy when he heard that each Time Warper gets their teleportation machine. "Wait, so does that mean I'm gonna get my teleporter, or do I have to keep this one?" spoke Max, barely able to contain his excitement. His uncle gave him a knowing look and instructed Max to follow him. They had entered a small, sophisticated part of the compound, and Max was surprised when his Uncle told him to hand over the watch strapped to his wrist. It felt weird taking it off. Max felt as if he were naked, defenceless. In the short time he had been wearing it, he felt it had become a part of him, an extension of his body. "So, what sort of design do you want? Remember, nothing too flashy or conspicuous. Try to keep it simple," Max's uncle said, looking at him with an inquisitive facial expression. This was going to be a hard decision for Max, and he had never really been good at making decisions, although Max did like the idea of a digital wristwatch. Yeah, yeah, that was a good idea. He had never had such clarity on a decision before. He could clearly see himself wearing it, and it would be small enough that it wouldn't stick out too badly among Romans, Egyptians, or whoever else he would encounter whilst on his time-travelling journey.

It was early morning. Max was dressed and ready. He wore what his Uncle called a battle suit. It consisted of a black unitard covered with armour plates and a black military-looking helmet. He had to wear this because they always had to expect the unexpected where they were going. One part of Max's costume was missing; if anything, it was the most important part—his watch. Yes, Max could call it his because it was made for him to be used by him. Max's Uncle pulled a long black rectangular box out of his backpack, carefully making sure not to drop it. He opened it and took out a sleek black and round wristwatch with two bands on either side to let Max strap it onto his wrist. Max wanted to relish this moment, for he knew that his life would forever change from the second he strapped that watch on. From the second he put that watch on, he would have to carry a burden that he could not share with anyone. Only he could carry

It couldn't be that bad, could it? I mean, you don't meet fourteen-year-olds who can time travel every day, do you?

This moment was one for the books. Max Junior's suit was finally complete. He felt like a superhero, but considering the circumstances, he should focus on more important matters, such as saving his Dad. Max's face was set like a stone, unmoving and unreadable. Fear and determination were etched across the crease lines on his forehead. He was ready.

CHAPTER 5

"Here we go again," thought Max as a wave of nausea swept over him. The world was spinning again, but this time, it was a lot faster, almost as if it had increased in strength. But getting to where Max and his uncle were going would take much power and energy. Max could feel his teleporter watch heating up on his wrist; it was getting so hot that it was now causing blisters. Max was worried that something had gone wrong until he stopped feeling everything.

"Max, get up, snap out of it. I need you here now!"

Max was awoken by a weird voice screaming in his ear. Slowly, he turned around to look at whatever woke him up and saw his Uncle's face, but he looked different. He had what looked like a scuba diving mouthpiece clamped between his teeth, but there was no oxygen tank on his back. How bizarre. Max felt something pushed between his teeth and realised his uncle was trying to force one of those mouthpieces between his tightly locked teeth. Understanding the assignment, he opened his mouth and let his Uncle place the mouthpiece between his teeth. Copying what his uncle was doing, Max clamped his teeth down hard. Max could suddenly see his surroundings with newfound clarity and understanding; he felt he could see the world in 4K ultra HD. The sleepiness he had felt just moments before had dissipated in an instant. Something was wrong, though. Max took some time to survey his surroundings and frowned. Initially, he thought they were in space, but now that he could see clearly, he realised there were no stars, moon, earth, sun, or other planets, only a dark brown murky space that engulfed and encased them on all sides.

"Dude, where are we?" asked Max, accidentally opening his mouth and releasing his mouthpiece, causing him to experience a wave of dizziness.

The air in this place was polluted, or there was no air. How bizarre.

"This is the in-between," mumbled Max's Uncle, more to himself than anything. "So, is this where we will find my dad?" asked Max, his voice laced with hope. Unfortunately for Max, his Uncle shook his head sadly.

"No, we have to get a special crystal from here that will give us the power to travel to your Father." Max sighed inwardly.

If he were standing on solid ground, he would have stomped his foot in frustration. Why did it take so long for him to see his Dad? He fumed. Why was everything stacked against him? Why did it have to be him? Couldn't it have been some other kid? His Uncle must have sensed his anger and laid a soothing hand on his shoulder.

"It's okay," he whispered gently into Max's ear. "We will find him if it's the last thing we do, but first, I need to tell you about the equipment we will use."

They spent about an hour discussing the equipment they would need to use during their trip. First was the rebreatherator, the mouthpiece Max and his Uncle had to keep in their mouths if they wanted to live through this ordeal. It recycled the polluted and intoxicated air that they breathed in and recycled it. To Max's shock, the second piece of equipment was a metre-long sword, like the one that Max had seen his Uncle wearing when he had first teleported to the Roman fort, but this one was slightly different. There was an array of different and multi-coloured buttons on the side of the hilt, and it was inside a black sheath that could be strapped around a person's waist. Max was surprised as his Uncle handed him one of the two swords with a grim expression. That wasn't why he was surprised; he was surprised that he would need any weapon. This must mean that finding his Dad would not be as easy as he thought. After everything was sorted, Max and his Uncle set off again; they had no time to waste. Maxwell Senior's life was at stake. Moving through this weird new terrain was difficult; there was nowhere to latch onto. The only way that Max was able to move forward was by swimming, and the only difference was that there was no water.

Finally, after hours of traversing through space and time, they had reached what looked like solid ground. Knowing that this may be the only solid ground they encounter throughout the rest of their journey, they seize their opportunity and land for a break. Normally, that would have been impossible because there was no gravity, and the patch of land they were on was not big enough to have its gravity. And that is one of the reasons why Max and his Uncle wore battle suits. Thanks to technology, they could stand up properly at the press of a button as if there was gravity. After a quick scan around their immediate area, Max and his Uncle could sit briefly and catch their breath. They had decided they deserved a break, but considering the circumstances, they had to compromise and say that they would rest for five minutes before they set off again, for they knew what was at stake and the consequences if they did not hurry. Boom! The ground shook. Max was first up, scanning the area, but he saw nothing. 'Where had that noise come from?'

he thought. He glanced at his Uncle from the corner of his eye; his eyes were wide open and alert. Max saw that he had drawn his sword and quickly followed suit. Boom! There it was again, louder this time. It was getting closer, but where was it coming from? The sound and the large dust around them were the only evidence that something was coming.

CHAPTER 6

"Roar!" It was behind them. Max whirled around, sword in hand, with a raging fire burning in his eyes and a fierce expression on his face, but what he saw transformed that expression into sheer terror and fear. In front of him stood a ten-foot gargantuan figure with a thick layer of pure muscle. It had the face of a beast with six eyes and four horns. Its body was covered in a small, grime-stained loincloth, but something weird was going on with whatever it was. Its body seemed to shift, looking like a giant spirit, a ghost, or a demon. The most disturbing part was its feet. When it became solid, its feet were covered in insects. Great black centipedes and weird blue slugs crawled across the surface, and the toes were that of snakes, long, ugly, and fat.

Phineas had always been a person who acted before thinking, and that had always gotten him into trouble, but he had never learned. So, without thinking, he charged straight for the giant beast, sword in hand. Before he had even taken two paces forward, he felt himself being flung into the air so hard that he lost consciousness before he even hit the ground, and when he did, he landed in a heap over two miles away from where he had been hit.

Max watched in horror as he saw the monster ghost lazily flick his hand and send his Uncle flying. Blackness clouded his vision; he could see nothing but his target.

His voice was devoid of all emotion when he said, "You made the wrong decision, mister. Now I'm coming for you."

During their short break, Uncle Phineas had taught Max some of the features of the sword he now carried. Turning on the vibration setting, Max ran at the beast, a roar coming out of his mouth so loud that the monster took a visible step backwards, a look of shock on its grotesque face. But before it could have a chance to regain its composure, Max was on top of it, plunging his sword straight into the beast's eye. "Aargh," the beast screamed in a frenzied attempt to dislodge the vibrating sword that had embedded itself into its eye. With one sharp twist, Max silenced the raging beast.

Max's vision cleared; it was no longer black. He looked at what he had done in awe; there was no way he had accomplished such a feat. Looking at himself, he realised he must have been fuelled by rage. That would explain the darkness he had seen. Uncle Phineas, where was he? Max had seen him flying but had not seen where he had landed. Max looked left and right, searching frantically until he saw a dark shape slumped over a mile away to his left.

"Wake up, Uncle Phineas, wake up."

Phineas woke up to the sound of his nephew, Max, shouting his name. Carefully, he opened his eyes but was instantly flooded with a torrent of pain. There was too much light, but where was it coming from? Too bright, he let himself fall back into the abyss of darkness.

Max looked around at the sound of his Uncle groaning and saw that he was attempting to sit up. Quickly, Max rushed to his aid, but as he bent down to help, he was fended off and given a dirty look. That was it. Max had had enough; he was tired of his uncle treating him like a little kid. "I just saved your behind, and you don't even show me a little gratitude. You act as if you're the one doing all the work, but you're wrong. I'm here as well. If my dad thought you could do this by yourself, he would have never gotten me involved, but he did, so deal with it!" Uncle Phineas looked taken aback, but Max didn't care. His Uncle had no right to treat him that way. If Max was going to help, he wanted to be treated like an adult, or at least a responsible fifteen, nearly sixteen-year-old.

Phineas stood up and glowered at his nephew, deep in thought. He seemed to have to forget his pride and treat this young man as an adult. Unexpectedly, Phineas stuck his hand out at his nephew. Max looked at that hand for a few seconds before enthusiastically grabbing it with his own and pumping it up and down. This was the start of a very special relationship.

Strategy, strategy, strategy. Max was getting tired of talking strategy. He wanted action. They had waited too long. What was supposed to be a five-minute pit stop had turned into an hour of talking and strategising, all the boring stuff.

Finally, after several long hours, Max and his Uncle prepared to depart, splitting all their supplies evenly: ten boil-in-a-bags each, with their weapons and spare clothes, and Uncle Phineas showed Max a special radio feature built into Max's watch. It could transmit over any distance, anywhere, because his watch contained a special crystal similar to the one they were trying to find that allowed them to travel in time. This would be essential once they embarked on their separate journeys. Max and his Uncle had both agreed that it was better to split up, which meant they could cover more ground in finding the crystals. There were three possible locations that the crystals could be in, so they would each go to one, and if they were unsuccessful, they would meet at the last location. Hopefully, it wouldn't have to come to that, but it was always smart to expect the unexpected.

Max embraced his Uncle in a deep hug, relishing the moment, but Uncle Phineas pulled away stiffly, tears forming in his eyes. He looked Max dead and said, "You're like a son to me. I promised your Dad that if anything ever happened to him, I would be there to protect you, so do me a favour and try to stay alive, will ya, kiddo? It would certainly keep me out of a lot of trouble." Max smiled at that and imagined his mother towering over Uncle Phineas with a livid look, making him chuckle. "Okay, Uncle Phineas, I promise to stay safe so that Mum doesn't beat the living daylights out of you." Uncle Phineas smiled, eradicating the dark bags under his eyes, if only for a moment. His face turned sour again as he clutched his chest in pain; he must've had at least one broken rib from when he had gotten hit and when he fell from the sky.

Max was feeling quite forlorn. It had been about 56 hours since he and his uncle parted ways, and Max was starting to feel like he was going crazy. He even caught himself talking to the air a few hours ago. It shows what being alone in a vast and empty space could do to a person. Max was close to his destination; he had about two days until he reached his intended destination, but considering there was no night or day, he had about forty-two hours left of journeying. So far, Max had only had about four breaks, so if he continued at his current pace, he would probably get to the crystal mine before his Uncle got to the salt lake that was supposedly crystal and mineral-rich, also one of the only places that you could find water, which was one of the reasons why that had not been the last place that they went to. Max had decided that he needed sleep if he were to carry on. His Uncle had given him a jet propulsion device, which meant that Max didn't have to swing his arms around like a madman anymore. That was a plus, but moving around in endless space would tire anyone out.

Activating the gravity feature, Max landed on a small piece of debris that looked like it had once been part of a small planet. "I wonder how this found its way here then," Max thought aloud. Too tired to care, Max unrolled his space tent. It was supposed to be large enough to fit a family, with a kitchen, bathroom, and an extra-large bedroom. Max looked at the small circular piece of metal in his hand, then remembered what his Uncle had shown him. There was no way that what he held in his hand was a tent. There must have been a mistake; his Uncle must have given him the wrong thing. How annoying. How was that?

"Max, Max, whatever you're doing, get up now. It's urgent," buzzed Max. He was lying on the cold, hard, and dirty ground, staring at what was possibly the sky, when he heard his Uncle's voice coming out of his bag. Scrambling up quickly, Max grabbed his small, chrome radio from his bag, frantically looking for the speak button. "Yes, Max here. What is it?" His heart was racing. What had happened, and had something gone wrong? Static, and then he heard his Uncle's voice again. "Well, I've received an emergency call from your father. It's not great news. He wants us to hurry up because the vortex he is in is closing up faster than before." Max's heart contracted in his chest; it was always surprise after surprise for Max. He could never catch a break. All this hard work. Was it worth it? Of course, it was. How could Max ever think of such a thing? It was his father they were talking about. Having been rekindled, the fire in Max's eyes shone brighter than ever before. Max spoke into the radio, his voice set. "I'm on my way to the first location. If I hurry, I should be there in three hours. I'll radio you to let you know once I'm there." Static, "If I leave now, I should be at location two by the time you get to location one."

"Over and out."

CHAPTER 7

Max was astounded by the beauty that surrounded him. He was in a cave in the middle of nowhere; the cave was just floating around, which was one reason why it had been so difficult for Max to find it. Due to its lack of foundation, it could come and go as it pleased; it was impossible to get a fixed location on it without placing a tracker, although that would not work because of all the interference from the crystals inside. Crystals of all sorts: red, green, blue, purple, and some were black, but only one of them was the crystal that Max needed. A sapphire crystal that was round in shape and small in size. Because of how small it was, it would have been tough to find if… Max had been given a frequency detector to detect the frequency of the special gem he was looking for. It worked a lot like a metal detector; in fact, most of the parts in that device had been from a metal detector. All Max had to do was run the frequency detector across the cave walls and along the floor. If the device detected even a trace of the sapphire crystal, it would start beeping insistently. Max pulled out the frequency detector and began scanning as fast as he could without missing a spot.

After hours of searching to no avail, Max finally accepted that he would not find the crystal he was looking for there. He sincerely doubted that his Uncle would find the crystal they were looking for either; there was no way they could be so lucky. No way at all.

Phineas' heart skipped a beat as the frequency detector he had held in his hand for ages, precariously scanning every nook and cranny, started to beep furiously in his hands.

Bending down, he began searching the ground for any sign of a round sapphire crystal. Not seeing anything, he started to dig. Unfortunately, he had not had the foresight to bring a digging kit, so he had to use his practically nonexistent fingernails. It was hard work. Phineas had always been a person who despised dirt. He had been the type of person who could not stand getting dirty, but he would do anything for his best friend, no matter the cost. If it had been anyone else, he would have tried to help them, but he would not have gone to such lengths to save them.

There it was, so close—just a bit more digging. Phineas could see the blue glint of the crystal. Turning on autopilot, he dug and dug and dug some more until enough of the crystal showed that he could pull it out with his fingers. Holding it in his hands, he felt a rush of giddiness and excitement. They could finally save his best friend, Max Senior. He was so full of excitement that he didn't even realise he had been hit on the back of the head until he fell to the ground, once again heading into the outstretched arms of oblivion. It had been a while since Max had last heard from his Uncle. They had agreed that if the crystal had not been found at the first two destinations, they would continue onto the last one together, but Max had not received any communication from his Uncle in the past two hours, so he had no idea what to do. The protocol was that if neither party received communication within four hours of the last transmission, the other party should proceed to the last location and not attempt any heroics or bravery. See, Max had always had a dislike for rules, especially ones that made no sense. There was no point in stupid rules, so he decided that he was going to go to wherever his Uncle was. Then, after that, he hoped that once he found his Uncle, he would also find the crystal if fate chose it to be so, but at the moment, the odds were not in his favour.

There was no way that Max would be able to match the speed at which his uncle was moving; it was just too fast. Even on its highest setting, the jet propulsion device could not excel him faster than 150mph without completely blowing its dual thrusters, but one pro was that Max felt no G-force. He could go insanely fast without the repercussions if the thrusters were more powerful. Max was seriously struggling to keep up; there was no way his Uncle could go that fast; it was just too far-fetched. The only plausible idea Max could devise was that some foul beast had snatched his Uncle.

His head spinning, Phineas searched for somewhere, anywhere to latch onto. He had been travelling at an insane speed for about an hour, but how, he knew not. Carefully, Phineas looked up at his captor: large, three eyes and a weird grin plastered onto its face, but other than that, there was nothing really that scary about it.

Finding his voice, Phineas whispered, "Who, what, where am I? Who are you? What are you?" He could not control his words; they just kept tumbling out of his mouth, so in the end, he realised it was better to keep his mouth shut.

"Calbi'gor saque."

With horror, Phineas realised that the creature was speaking to him in a language he did not understand.

"Pardon," was all he could say in response.

How could he escape this woeful predicament if he couldn't communicate with the foul beast? Looking confused, the beast—

who Phineas had decided looked like a person named Gor—stepped back and fiddled with a small black rectangular block on its neck.

"Hallo, human."

Phineas stared in amazement. Gor had just spoken English, but how? Puzzled, Phineas looked at the rectangular block that Gor had just been playing with; it was attached to his neck with what was that, a daisy chain? Putting two and two together, Phineas realised that Gor had some device that allowed him to speak different languages. The science of it was way too complex and way ahead of time for the current human species back on earth, which meant that Gor, the deformed-looking creature looming over him, had created it himself, proving his extraordinary intellect.

Max circled around his Uncle's location. Looking below him, he saw a house, an actual house, fully furnished and all. The only odd thing about it was that it was completely alone, just floating around by itself, totally and utterly alone. Landing on the porch steps, Max pulled out his sword and put his game face on; he would not leave this building without his Uncle and the crystal. Max searched every nook and cranny of the house, tiptoeing as quietly as he could, but as he stood outside what seemed like the master bedroom, he could hear two voices. One was the voice of his Uncle, deep and filled with authority. The other was the opposite, high and squeaky but laced with timidity. Preparing himself to break into the room, Max counted to three. 1…2…

"HI!"

Without warning, the door to the bedroom had been flung open, and standing over Max was a very, very ugly-looking… thing. That was the only way to describe it. The only difference between this thing and the monster that had nearly killed Max's Uncle was that it was not scary; apart from its extreme ugliness, it looked cute with its crooked smile and mismatched eyes.

"Max, I was wondering when you would appear, " Phineas said.

He watched as his nephew's eyes lit up upon hearing his voice. "Uncle, you're alive!" Max got off the floor, onto which he had fallen when Gor opened the bedroom door.

Phineas winked at Maxwell Junior and said with a mischievous grin plastered on his face, "I think it's about time we bring your Dad home, don't you?"

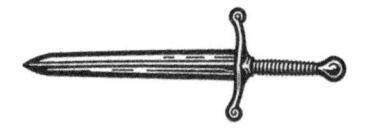

CHAPTER 8

All the necessary gear was prepared; they were ready. It was time to bring Maxwell Senior back home.

The friendly alien monster Gor had helped cut the crystal Uncle Phineas had mined into three slightly less powerful crystal shards small enough to be slotted into the small hatch at the bottom of their time-travelling devices. Turning to look at each other, Max and Phineas nodded; talking was not an option. Gor had also created three masks that could be put over their faces to provide a constant supply of oxygen, much more effective than Phineas's mouthpiece design.

Due to the unpredictable nature of the crystal shards, Max and his uncle split their necessary supplies into three packs: one for Max, one for his uncle, and the last one for Max's father, Maxwell Senior. Since there was no guarantee that they would be together when they travelled to the time void where Max Senior was imprisoned, they were to rendezvous at Max Senior's location and keep in contact the entire time. It had been decided that Max would be carrying his father's equipment. Uncle Phineas had come to this conclusion simply because Max was younger and more agile than him, so he was likely to find Max Senior first.

If Max Senior wore his watch, Max Junior and his Uncle could pinpoint his location and head straight to him, but that was if he was still alive.

Max and his Uncle simultaneously pressed the clock function on their watches. Max winced, preparing for the searing pain that was to come, except it didn't. Instead, a deathly cold, tingly sensation embraced his wrist. It hurt so badly that Max was on the verge of passing out.

Into the void they went.

Max woke up sometime later. He opened his eyes: nothing. He tried wiping his mask, but nothing. Slowly, he reached into the pack on his back and pulled out his torch. It was supposed to emit a super powerful beam of light illuminating anything up to a mile away, but Max Junior could only see things in the immediate vicinity. He couldn't even see his hand if he held it too far away. As its name suggests, this time void was completely devoid of light.

Max was completely lost; he had no idea what to do next. Was he supposed to go to his Uncle or just stay put? It was as if his memory had been wiped clean. That was until he saw a head, a decapitated human head.

Whose head was it? Max wondered. He gently floated towards it, making sure not to get too close. The facial features looked familiar, too familiar. The sharp upward curve of the nose with an obvious double chin and two dark and dull lifeless eyes. Max knew this person; it was the head of his grandfather, Bartholomew Eduardo Alexander. He had died about ten years ago in an unfortunate car accident. Max Junior knew this because he had been there while his grandfather was on his deathbed. He had held his hand as his soul drifted away. So, whose head was this in front of him then? Max started when the severed head's eyes opened and started swivelling left to right, up and down. Max stared in horrified silence as the head began to open its mouth, with its cracked and bloody lips showing the few rotten brown teeth that it had left. Maxwell Junior began to quake as the weird severed head began to float toward him; he couldn't move; his body was completely frozen. It came closer until it stopped before Max's face and SNAP.

Max opened his eyes, and it was gone. The decapitated head was gone; seconds before, it had been about to bite Max's nose off, and now it had just disappeared. Max looked around warily, trying to see through the intense darkness, but as expected, his attempts were futile.

After a couple of useless, nonsensical minutes, Max had finally regained his wits and opened up the tracking function on his watch. He could see two dots: one red dot and one blue dot that was quickly closing in on the red dot that appeared to be flashing, which indicated a critical condition. That wasn't good, not good at all. Judging by the speed of the blue dot, Max guessed that it was his Uncle Phineas, which meant that the flashing red dot was Max's father. It was time for Max Junior to get a move on.

"Max, you need to hurry up, kiddo. No pressure, but your Dad doesn't have very long left," Max's watch beeped as he received his uncle's transmission.

Max responded with a short and swift "Roger," for Max was only a few minutes away from being reunited with his father; nothing would stop him. Well, that was until he saw his Uncle pop up in front of him, about a centimetre away, with a murderous look full of malice and hate that was directed right at Max.

Phineas glared at his so-called nephew. He had not shown it before but hated Max and his father passionately. All because of one woman: Max's mother.

When Maxwell Senior and his best friend Phineas Augustus were wee boys, they were inseparable; they would never be apart until one day, Phineas met a girl named Anne

Parker. She had the looks and the personality. Phineas loved Anne with all his heart, but unfortunately, his feelings were not reciprocated. So, one day, when Phineas introduced his new girlfriend to his best friend, it was love at first sight. A spark lit up within Anne when she set her eyes on Maxwell, and they slowly grew closer and closer until, five years later, they finally got married. That was the day Phineas snapped. He became so overwhelmed with hatred for Maxwell Senior, and when Maxwell Junior was born, Phineas made it his life mission to get Anne back, and he was willing to do anything to achieve that goal. Because Phineas was also a high-ranked time warper, he had almost unlimited access to time dimensions and a few time voids. He had created the perfect plan to trap Max Senior and his son. All he had to do was program Max Senior's watch to a certain location and disable the travelling function once he reached that location, in this case, the time void. The second part of his plan would be to assist the son in finding his father and then trap him in the void. It had been a foolproof plan then, but now Phineas started re-evaluating his situation. It looked as if his nephew wasn't going down without a fight.

As a resilient young man, Max knew that something was going on. He looked at his Uncle before him and very nearly decided to give up, but he would've if it were only him; his father's life was also on the line here, and there was no way he was going to give up that easily. It was one of his greatest flaws.

"All you need to do is lay down your weapon and come with me; nobody gets hurt." It was hard for Max to listen to Uncle Phineas when he had just said one of the most used phrases in any action movie. He couldn't hold it in any longer, so he let out a massive snort of laughter.

Phineas looked at Max quizzically. Had he just laughed? Did he think this was some kind of joke? "I said, "GIVE ME YOUR SWORD!" Phineas was beginning to lose his cool; things were not going as smoothly as he had wanted them to go. Why, why, why? Phineas was losing his marbles. He had enough; his nephew was not taking him seriously. His cocky smile made Phineas want to throw him a hundred miles away.

Max had no idea what he was doing, but he knew it was driving his uncle nuts. He was twitching and shaking; there was no way that he was okay. He looked like he needed some real help. There was no other way to explain it. What normal person kidnaps their best friend and his son, then tries to trap them in a completely different dimension? You had to be bonkers to even think about such a thing. It just wasn't normal. Max wasn't even surprised when his uncle Phineas pulled out his sword, but this was different. It was black, pure black. It was so black that it completely blended in with the surroundings. The man standing in front of Max was not the uncle he had grown to know; the person in front of him was a psychopath gone beyond recognition. Reluctantly, Max pulled his sword out of its sheath on his hip and prepared himself mentally and physically to fight right until the end. Giving up wasn't even an option.

CHAPTER 9

The only time Max had ever used a real sword was when he was fighting The Beast while searching for the time crystal in between. He still didn't know what had happened back then; something weird had clicked inside him, turning on autopilot. Max realised that the only way to escape his current predicament was to tap into that auto mode. Right now, the best thing that Max could do was weave, dodge, and block. It was clear that Uncle

Phineas had spent a long time training; his form was amazing, but even so, it still had minor flaws. Somehow, Max noticed them; every time Phineas jabbed, he left his right side open and prone to attack.

Max realised that if he exploited the gap in his Uncle's defences, the battle would be over quickly and with minimal damage. It was also the only way because, by now, Max was covered in green bruises and had plenty of small nicks and cuts from where his Uncle had managed to get through his defences. Max had to choose his moment carefully; it was like chess sometimes; you must sacrifice to win.

Now! Max saw a small gap on his Uncle's right side and struck.

Phineas looked at the young man floating before him, then slowly tilted his head downward to see the metre-long bronze sword jutting from his side. It was a gruesome sight, and because of the lack of gravity, the blood from the wound flowed upward in small bubbles.

Without looking up, Phineas said, "Well done, boy. You did well. I never expected to beat you because you're skilled beyond imagination like your father." Max was startled.

Why would his uncle go through all this if he knew what would happen? It made no sense to him. "Some things are better left a mystery, boy. Now, go find your father." Max blinked back tears. This man, who had been his uncle, his mentor, and also the man who had tried to kill him, was now… gone?

Uncle Phineas was gone, just vanished. He had been there a second ago; now, he was gone. The only thing that remained of him was his congealed blood that had attached itself to Max's sword. 'Find your father.' Those had been his Uncle's last words, and that was what Max would do.

CHAPTER 10

Maxwell Senior had done the one thing he had always told himself not to do. He had given in. He had been clinging to one small hope: the hope that his son would come, that his son would free him from his grotesque prison. There were bones scattered everywhere. Maxwell could smell the death in the air; it was an ominous, putrid smell.

"He will come for me; I know he will. He has to come." Those were the thoughts that had kept Max Senior alive until this moment, the words that had kept his heart beating.

When Max was imprisoned by his best friends, he realised his cell had been on hope. The black, vapoury walls leeched all hope that the person imprisoned inside had, and after all your hope had been sucked away, you would become like one of the many bones that were scattered across the dark, misty floor. Maxwell could feel it happening: his hair fell in chunks, and his vision blurred. The still rational part of his mind reckoned that he only had a maximum of two hours before his body would start fully decomposing.

"There's nothing here!" Max exclaimed.

He was getting well and truly worked up. It was already impossible to see anything through the darkness, and on top of that, an ominous mist had engulfed everything within a hundred-mile radius. It made Max Junior want to rip his eyes out because, at this point, there was no need for them; they did nothing to help him see anyway.

Maxwell Junior had never been scared of anything. That was until the day he turned ten.

On December 31st, 2009, Maxwell Junior

told his mother and father he would play at the park across the street with his friends. His parents had been extremely reluctant to let him go because of the thick blanket of fog covering the entire neighbourhood. Still, they had eventually agreed, given that it was Max's birthday. Max couldn't see or hear anything when he arrived at the park. He said that he would wait for five minutes, but he began seeing weird things in the fog, weird beings that he couldn't make out. They were moving closer and closer, so close that Max involuntarily let out a cry of fear and ran as fast as his beanpole legs could go. He didn't stop until he had safely closed and locked the door to his room. As Maxwell Junior stared down into the mist, all those memories came flooding back to him, making him want to curl up into a ball and cry until his father came to rescue him.

"But that's the thing. I have to rescue my father; otherwise, he will never be able to rescue me."

Max realised that the only way he would go through the mist without falling unconscious was to think about his father and everything he had done to help the world and his family.

It was now or never. Even though Max was wearing his special mask and battle suit, he was finding it incredibly hard to navigate through the thick mist. It didn't want to let him through, pushing against him. Why, he wondered. Why was the whole universe working against him? It wasn't fair; he only wanted to find his father.

"Dear God, I know that I have not always made the right choices in life, but right now, I need to find my dad and save him before he dies. So, if you could help and give me strength and courage, it would help me greatly. Amen."

Max frowned inwardly.

Where had that come from? Yes, his father may be a preacher, but Maxwell Junior had never really paid attention or cared about all that God stuff. But now, as he felt an immense aura of what could only be described as supernatural strength to keep going, the mist was no longer an issue. It almost seemed to part as he went through it, and in no time, Max could make out the faint outline of a small black box floating around. It was weird, though; the closer Max got to it, the more he wanted to give up, just turn around and leave.

In fact, he had turned a full one hundred and eighty degrees before he came to his senses and realised that he had not come this far just to give up. No, he would continue, no matter how scared he was. He also knew that God was watching over him somewhere in heaven, and it gave Max the courage to keep going until he reached the door that separated him from his dad. He had no idea what to do now. From the little Max could see, there was no visible way to open the door. Cautiously, Max stretched out his index finger to touch the door slowly. Max barely had time to move to the side before the door swung open, and inside, Max saw his father, but he was a skeleton. His skin hung off him, and his eyes looked like they were engraved into his skull, devoid of all signs of life.

"No, go away, you're not real. Leave me alone."

Max heard his father's hoarse voice, barely louder than a whisper. It pained Max to see his father, the great Maxwell Senior, in such a terrible, beaten-up, and vulnerable state, but there was only one way to heal him.

"Dad, it's me, Max. I'm real. It's time to go home."

Maxwell Junior quickly closed the distance between him and his father, gently enclosed his hand around his father's fragile wrist, and turned the side button on his watch backwards. As the blue time vortex opened up, Max glanced sideways at his father and saw a faint spark of light in his father's eyes. He knew at that very moment Maxwell Senior would recover.

ABOUT THE AUTHOR

I'm Micaiah, and I'm 14 years old at the time of writing this book. I've always loved reading books since I was a toddler and preferred receiving books as gifts instead of toys. English has always been one of my more favourable school subjects. I grew up in South-West London, Kingston, with my mother. We had a close relationship even back then. I grew up without a male figure to guide me, but I had my mum and grandmother, who are strong and important figures in my life, and I don't think that I would be the person I am right now without her love and guidance. Growing up in mainstream schools,

I always felt as if I didn't fit in, but I always knew I had a talent that I hadn't tapped into yet. I strongly feel my sense of belonging is with fellow writers and authors.

It has always been my greatest ambition to meet and stand with the likes of Malorie Blackman, Suzanne Collins, Rick Riordan, Anthony Horowitz, to name a few authors, for their breathtakingly amazing work.

And finally, my biggest dream is to get people like me, young and old alike, to take reading seriously. You can be cool and still read. Age should not be a barrier to reading and writing books.

Printed in Great Britain
by Amazon